The Legend of the
HOLY DRINKER

THE LEGEND OF THE
HOLY DRINKER

Joseph Roth

Translated by Michael Hofmann

Granta Books
London

Granta Publications, 2/3 Hanover Yard, London N1 8BE

First published in Great Britain by Granta Books 2000
This edition published by Granta Books 2001
Originally published in German as *Die Legende vom heiligen Trinker*,
1939

A CIP catalogue record for this book
is available from the British Library.

1 3 5 7 9 10 8 6 4 2

Printed and bound in Great Britain by Mackays of Chatham plc

1

On a spring evening in 1934 a gentleman of mature years descended one of the flights of stone steps that lead from the bridges over the Seine down to its banks. It is there that, as all the world knows and so will hardly need reminding, the homeless poor of Paris sleep, or rather spend the night.

One such poor vagrant chanced to be walking towards the gentleman of mature years, who was incidentally well-dressed and had the appearance of a visitor, disposed to take in the sights of foreign cities. This vagrant looked no less pitiable and bedraggled than any other, but to the elderly well-dressed man he seemed to merit some particular attention: why, we are unable to say.

It was, as already mentioned, evening, and under the bridges on the banks of the river it was rather darker than it was up on the bridges and embankments above. The vagrant was swaying slightly and was clearly the worse for wear. He seemed not to have noticed the elderly, well-dressed gentleman. He, though, had clearly seen the swaying man from some way off, and, far from swaying himself, was striding purposefully towards him. He seemed intent on barring the way of the seedy man. They both came to a halt and confronted one another.

'Where are you going, brother?' asked the elderly, well-dressed gentleman.

The other looked at him for a moment, and said: 'I wasn't aware that I had a brother, and I don't know where I'm going.'

'Then I will try to show you the way,' said the gentleman. 'But first will you not be angry with me if I ask you for a rather unusual favour?'

'I am entirely at your service,' said the clochard.

'I can see that you are not without blemish. But God has sent you to me. Now, if you'll forgive my saying so, I am sure you could use some money. I have more than enough. Could you tell me how much you require? At least for the immediate future?'

The other reflected for a moment and said: 'Twenty francs.'

'That can't be enough,' replied the gentleman. 'I'm sure you require two hundred.'

The vagrant took a step back, and for a moment it looked as if he might fall over, but he managed to stay on his feet, if with a little local difficulty. Then he said: 'Certainly, I would rather two hundred francs than twenty, but I am a man of honour. You may not have realised as much. I am unable to accept the sum you offer me for the following reasons: firstly, because I don't have the pleasure of knowing you; secondly, because I don't know how and when I would be able to repay you; and thirdly, because there would be no possibility of your asking me to repay you. I have no address. Almost every day finds me under a different bridge. And yet, in spite of that, as I have assured you, I am a man of honour, albeit of no fixed address.'

'I too have no address,' replied the elderly gentleman, 'and I too may be found under a different bridge every day, and yet I would ask you please to accept the two hundred francs — a bagatelle for a man such as yourself. And as regards its repayment, I should explain why I am unable to refer you, say, to a bank, where you could deposit the money in my account. The fact is that I have recently become a Christian, as a result of reading the story of little St Thérèse de Lisieux. I have a special reverence for her little statue in the Chapelle de Sainte Marie des Batignolles, which you will have no trouble in finding. Therefore, when you next happen to have two hundred francs, and your conscience will not allow you to go on owing me such a paltry sum, I would ask you to go to Sainte Marie des Batignolles, and to leave the money in the hands of the priest who reads the Mass there. For if you owe it to anyone, you owe it to little Thérèse. Don't forget now: Sainte Marie des Batignolles.'

'I see,' said the clochard, 'that you have understood me and my sense of honour perfectly. I give you my word that I will keep my word. But I am only able to go to Mass on a Sunday.'

'By all means, on a Sunday,' said the elderly gentleman. He took two hundred francs from his wallet, gave them to the swaying fellow, and said: 'I thank you!'

'It was a pleasure,' replied the other, and immediately vanished into the depths of the gloom.

For it had grown dark in the meantime, down by the river, while up above, on the bridges and quays, the silvery lamps were lighting up, to proclaim the merry Parisian night.

2

The well-dressed gentleman also vanished into the darkness. He had indeed experienced the miracle of faith. He had made up his mind to lead a life of poverty. And therefore he lived under bridges.

As for the other fellow, though, he was a drunkard and a toper. His name was Andreas. He lived, like many drunkards, a rather fortuitous existence. It was a long time since he had last had two hundred francs. And perhaps because it was such a long time, he took out a scrap of paper and a stub of pencil, and by the sparse light of one of the few lamps under one of the bridges, he noted down the address of St Thérèse, and the sum of two hundred francs that he now owed her. Then he climbed one of the flights of steps that lead from the Seine's banks to the quays. He knew there was a restaurant there. And he went in, and ate and drank plentifully, and he spent a lot of money, and when he left he took a whole bottle with him for the night, which he intended to spend under the bridge, as usual. Yes, and he picked up a newspaper from a wastepaper bin, not in order to read it, but to wrap himself up in it. For, as all vagrants know, newspapers keep you warm.

3

The following morning, Andreas got up rather earlier than usual, for he had slept unusually well. After pondering the matter for a long time, he remembered that he had experienced a miracle yesterday, a miracle. And as it had been a mild night and he seemed to have slept particularly well wrapped up in his newspaper, better than for some time, he decided he would go down to the river and wash, something he hadn't done for many months, in fact not since the onset of the colder weather.

Before beginning to undress, though, he felt in the left inside pocket of his jacket, where, if he remembered correctly, there ought still to be some tangible evidence of the miracle. Then he set about looking for a secluded spot on the banks of the Seine, so that he might at least wash his face and neck. However, embarrassed at finding himself in plain view of people, of poor people such as himself (derelicts, as he now suddenly thought of them), he quickly abandoned his original plan, and made do with merely dipping his hands into the water. Then he put his jacket on again, felt once more for the banknote in his left inside pocket, and, feeling thoroughly cleansed, yes, positively transformed, he set forth.

He set forth into the day, into one of his typical days, such as he had now been passing since the beginning of time, resolved once more to direct his steps to the familiar Rue des Quatre Vents, to the Russian-Armenian restaurant Tari-Bari, where he was in the habit of investing in cheap liquor whatever little money had come his way.

But, at the first newspaper kiosk he passed, he stopped, attracted initially by the illustrations on the covers of some of the weekly magazines, but then also suddenly gripped by curiosity to learn what day it was today, what date and what day of the week. So he bought himself a newspaper, and saw that it was a Thursday, and he suddenly remembered that the day on which he was born was also a Thursday, and, regardless of the date, he decided to make this particular Thursday his birthday. And, already full of a childish feeling of excitement and celebration, he decided unhesitatingly to follow some good, yes, some noble prompting, and for once not go to the Tari-Bari, but instead, newspaper in hand, seek out some classier establishment, where he would order a roll and some coffee – perhaps inspirited with a jigger of rum.

So, proudly, in spite of his tattered clothing, he walked into a respectable bistro and sat down at a table – he, who for so long had only stood at bars, or rather propped his elbow on them. He sat. And since his chair was facing a mirror, he could hardly avoid looking at his

13

reflection in it, and it was as though he were making his own acquaintance again after a long absence. He was shocked. Immediately he realised why for the last few years he had been so distrustful of mirrors. It was not good to see evidence of his own dissipation with his own eyes. For as long as he had been able to avoid seeing it, it was either as though he had no face at all, or still had the old one from the time before he had become dissipated.

Now, though, he was shocked, especially when he compared his own physiognomy with those of the sleek and respectable men who were seated round him. It was fully a week since he had last had a shave — a rough and ready one, as was usually the case, administered to him by one of his fellows, who would occasionally agree to shave a brother-vagrant for a few coppers. Now, though, in view of his decision to begin a new life, nothing less than a real shave would do. He decided to go to a proper barber's shop before going on with his breakfast.

He suited the action to the thought, and went to a barber.

When he returned to the bistro, he found his former place occupied, and he was now only able to get a distant view of himself in the mirror. But it was enough for him to see that he had been smartened up, rejuvenated, become a new man. Yes, his face seemed to be giving off a sort of radiance which made the tattiness of his clothes seem irrelevant – the ripped shirt-front, and the red-and-white striped foulard he wound over his frayed collar.

So he sat down again, our Andreas, and in the spirit of his renewal he ordered his 'café, arrosé rhum', in the confident tone of voice that had long ago once been his, and which now returned to him, like an old sweetheart. The waiter served him, he thought, with a show of esteem that was only accorded to respectable guests. This particularly gratified our Andreas – it boosted his self-esteem, and strengthened him in the conviction that today was indeed his birthday.

A gentleman, who had been sitting alone at a table close to that of our clochard, had been studying him for a

while, and now turned to him and addressed him as fol-
lows: 'Would you be interested in earning some money?
You could do some work for me. You see, we're moving
house tomorrow. You could help my wife and the removal
men. You look as though you have the strength for it. Are
you free tomorrow? Would you like to?'

'Yes, by all means,' replied Andreas.

'And how much would you expect to be paid for
two days' work? Tomorrow and Saturday. Because, you
see, I've got rather a large flat, and the one we're moving
into is even bigger. There's stacks of furniture too. I won't
be able myself to help, as I'll be busy looking after the
shop.'

'I'm just the man for the job!' said the vagrant.

'Would you care for a drink?' asked the gentleman.

And he ordered two Pernods, they clinked glasses,
the gentleman and Andreas, and they also fixed the rate
for the job: it was to be two hundred francs.

'Shall we have another?' asked the gentleman, after
finishing his Pernod.

'Yes, but let me buy this one,' said the vagrant Andreas. 'You don't know me, but I'm a man of principle. An honest worker. Take a look at my hands!' — and he held out his hands for inspection — 'They may be dirty and calloused, but they're real working-man's hands.'

'That's what I like to see!' said the gentleman. He had twinkling eyes, a pink plump baby face and, smack in the middle of it, a little black moustache. All in all, he was a friendly chap, and Andreas took a liking to him.

So they drank together, and Andreas paid for the second round. And when the baby-faced man got up, Andreas saw that he was extremely fat. He took a visiting-card from his wallet, and wrote his address on it. And then he took a hundred-franc note from the same wallet, and handed both together to Andreas, saying: 'To be sure you'll turn up tomorrow! Tomorrow morning at eight, all right? Don't forget! I'll pay you the rest when you're finished! And then we'll have another aperitif together! All right? Cheerio, friend!' And with that he was gone, the fat gentleman with the baby face, and nothing surprised

Andreas more than the fact that he had produced his address from the same pocket as his money. Well, seeing as *he* now had some money, and the prospect of more to come, he decided to buy a wallet himself. With this in mind, he set off in search of a leather-goods shop. In the first such shop he came across, he saw a young sales girl. He thought she looked very attractive, the way she stood behind the counter, wearing a black dress with a white apron tied across her bosom, the mop of curls on her head and the heavy gold bracelet on her right wrist. He took his hat off to her, and said breezily: 'I'm looking for a wallet.' The girl cast a cursory glance at his tattered clothing, not in any spirit of disapproval, simply to assess the customer in front of her. Because in her shop, she sold wallets that were expensive, moderately expensive and very cheap. Without any more ado, she climbed up a ladder and took down a box from the topmost shelf. That was where those wallets were kept that customers sometimes brought in, in part-exchange for new ones. Andreas happened to notice that the girl had very shapely legs, and that her feet were in very trim little shoes, and he remembered those half-forgotten times when he himself had stroked such calves and kissed such feet. The faces he had forgotten, he had no recollection of the faces of the women – with one single exception, namely the one for whose sake he had gone to prison. In the meantime, the girl climbed down from the ladder, and opened the box, and he picked one of the wallets that were lying at the very top, barely looking at it. He paid, put his hat back on, and smiled at the girl and the girl smiled back at him. Rather absent-mindedly, he put the new wallet in his pocket, beside his money. It suddenly seemed to have no point, this wallet. On the other hand, the ladder and the legs and feet of the girl filled his mind. Therefore he directed his steps towards Montmartre, in search of those places where he had once found pleasure. In a narrow and steep little lane, he found the bar where the girls were. He sat down at a table with several of them, bought a round of drinks, and chose one of the girls, in fact the one who was sitting next to him. They went up to her room. And even though it was only afternoon, he slept until the following morning – and, because the *patronne* was feeling generous, she let him sleep on.

That morning, the Friday, he went to work for the fat gentleman. His job was to help the lady of the house to pack, and, even though the furniture removal men were doing their work, there was more than enough, both arduous and less arduous, to keep Andreas busy. In the course of the day, he felt the strength returning to his muscles, and he took pleasure in his work. He had grown up working, he had been a coal-miner like his father, and briefly a farmer like his father before him. If only the lady of the house hadn't got on his nerves so much, giving him pointless instructions, telling him to be in two places at once, so that he didn't know whether he was coming or going. But he could appreciate that she was agitated too. It couldn't have been easy for her, moving house just like that, and maybe she wasn't sure about the new place either. She stood there dressed to go out, in coat and hat and gloves, with her handbag and umbrella, even though she must have known that she would be remaining in the old house all that day and night, and even some of the next day as well. From time to time she would paint her lips, and that too Andreas could well understand. Naturally – she was a lady.

Andreas worked all day. When he had finished, the lady of the house said to him: 'Come punctually at seven o'clock tomorrow.' She took a little purse full of coins from her handbag. Her fingers scrabbled about in it for a long time, picking up a ten-franc piece then dropping it again, before settling instead on a five-franc piece. 'Here's a little something for you!' she said. 'But,' she added, 'you're not to spend it all on drink, and be sure to be here in good time tomorrow!'

Andreas thanked her, left and spent the money – but no more – on drink. He spent the night in a small hotel.

He was woken up at six in the morning. And he went to work feeling fresh and alert.

4

He arrived even before the removal men. The lady of the house was already standing there, exactly as on the previous day, in hat and gloves, as though she hadn't gone to bed at all, and she said to him pleasantly: 'I can see you took my advice, and didn't spend the whole of your tip on drink.'

Andreas got to work. Later he went with the lady to the new house they were moving into, and waited till the friendly man came home, and paid him the second instalment of his wage.

'Now for that drink I promised you,' said the gentleman. 'Let's go.'

But the lady of the house wouldn't allow it, she stood between them and said to her husband: 'Dinner's ready.' And so Andreas went away alone, and that evening he ate and drank alone, and afterwards he visited another couple of bars. He drank a lot, but he didn't get drunk, and he was careful not to spend too much money, because the next day, mindful of his promise, he wanted to go to the Chapelle de Sainte Marie des Batignolles, and pay at least some of his debt to little Thérèse. But he did drink just enough to cloud his judgement, and make him lose his pauper's infallible instinct for the very cheapest hotel in the *quartier*.

So he went into a slightly more expensive hotel, where, because he had no luggage, and his clothes were in a poor state, he was made to pay in advance. But he wasn't bothered by that, and he slept peacefully until the following morning. He was woken up by the sound of bells tolling in a nearby church, and straight away it came to him what an important day it was today: it was Sunday, and he had to go to little Thérèse and pay his debt. He quickly pulled his clothes on, and hurried over to the square where the church was. Even so, he reached it too late, because when he arrived the congregation was just emerging from the church after the ten o'clock service. He asked when the next Mass would begin, and was told at noon. He felt at a bit of a loose end, standing around outside the church. There was a whole hour to wait, and he would have preferred not to spend it on the street. So he looked around for some place where he might wait in greater comfort, and saw a bistro diagonally across the square from the church, and decided to spend the hour till Mass there instead.

With the assurance of a man who knows he has money in his pocket, he ordered a Pernod, and with the assurance of a man who has drunk a good many of them in the course of his life, he drank it. He drank another, and a third, adding less water each time. By the time the fourth was served to him, he had no idea whether he had had two glasses, or five or even six. Nor could he remember what he was doing in this café or in this part of town. All he knew was that there was some obligation he had to discharge, some honourable obligation, and he paid, got up, and had walked steadily out of the door when he caught sight of the church facing him across the square, and remembered in a flash where he was and why and to accomplish what. He was just about to take a step towards the church when he suddenly heard the sound of his name. A voice was calling 'Andreas!', a woman's voice. It reached him from another age. He stopped and turned his head to the right, where the voice was coming from. And straight away he recognised the face for whose sake he had gone to prison. It was Caroline.

Caroline! She was wearing clothes and a hat he had never seen her in before, but it was still the same face, and he threw himself into her arms, which she had quickly opened wide to receive him. 'What a coincidence,' she said. And it was really her voice, the voice of Caroline.

'Are you on your own?' she asked.

'Yes,' he said, 'I'm alone.'

'Come on then, we need to have a talk,' she said.

'But, but,' he replied, 'I've got a rendezvous.'

'With a woman?' she asked.

'Yes,' he said timidly.

'Who with?'

'With little Thérèse,' he replied.

'Never mind her,' said Caroline.

Just at that moment a taxi drove by, and Caroline stopped it by waving her umbrella at it. She gave the cabbie an address, and before Andreas quite realised what was happening, he was sitting in the cab with Caroline, driving away, racing away, as it seemed to Andreas, going through a mixture of familiar and unfamiliar streets, to God knows where!

They left the city altogether, and stopped in a land-scape, or rather in front of a cultivated garden that was pale green, the green of spring to come. There was a discreet restaurant tucked away behind some almost leafless trees.

Caroline got out first; with her familiar rapacious steps, she got out first, clambering over his knees. She paid, and he followed her. They went into the restaurant and sat side by side on a bench upholstered in green velvet, as in younger days, before he'd gone to prison. She ordered for them both, as she always did; she looked at him and he was afraid to look at her.

'Where have you been all this time?' she asked.

'All over the place,' he said. 'Nowhere really. I've only been back at work again for two days. All the time we didn't see each other I was drinking and sleeping under bridges like a clochard. I expect you've had a better life. With men,' he added, after a pause.

'You can talk,' she retorted. 'Drunk and out of work and sleeping under bridges you may be, but somehow you still find the time and the opportunity to meet this Thérèse of yours. If I hadn't happened to come along, I expect you'd have gone off with her.'

He made no reply, and in fact said nothing at all until they had both finished their meat course, and the cheese had arrived, and the fruit. Just as he was emptying his glass of wine, he was again gripped by the sudden feeling of panic that he had so often felt when he was living with Caroline, years ago. Again, he felt like running away from her, and he called out: 'Waiter, the bill please!' But she quickly cut in: 'No, waiter, that's my affair!' The waiter, a wise man who had been around, said: 'I heard the gentleman call first.' And so it was Andreas who paid. He took all the money from his left inside jacket pocket, and after paying, he saw with horror – somewhat diminished by the wine he had drunk – that he no longer had the full sum he owed the little saint. But then again, he comforted himself, so many miracles are happening to me these days, just one after another, that surely I'll be able to get the money together and pay her back next week.

'So, I see you're a rich man,' said Caroline when they were outside. 'I suppose you've got that little Thérèse working for you?'

Again, he made no reply, and so she was convinced that her suspicion was well founded. She demanded to be taken to the cinema. He took her to the cinema. It was the first film he'd seen in ages. In fact it was so long since he'd seen one that he could barely follow it, and he fell asleep on Caroline's shoulder. Then they went on to a dance-hall where there was an accordionist, and it was so long since he'd last danced that he didn't know how to dance properly any more when he took to the floor with Caroline. Other dancers kept cutting in and taking her away from him, for she was still young and desirable. He sat by himself at a table and drank Pernod, and it felt just like old times, when Caroline would go off dancing with other men, and he would sit and drink by himself. Finally he had had enough, and he got up, pulled her violently away from her partner, and said: 'We're going home now!' He gripped her neck, refused to let go, and paid and went home with her. She lived nearby.

It was all just like old times again, just like the old times before he'd gone to prison.

5

He woke up very early in the morning. Caroline was still asleep. A solitary bird twittered outside the open window. He lay there for a while with open eyes, no more than a couple of minutes. During those minutes he was thinking. It seemed to him that not for a long time had so many remarkable things happened to him as now, in the space of this single week. He turned his head abruptly and saw Caroline lying beside him. He saw what he had failed to notice yesterday, at their meeting: that she had aged; pale and puffy and breathing heavily, she slept on into the morning like a woman past her best. He recognised the changes wrought by the years, which seemed to have passed him by. But he also felt the changes in his heart, and he decided to get up immediately, without waking Caroline, and to leave just as fortuitously, or rather just as fatefully, as the two of them had run into one another yesterday. He quietly dressed and went off, into another day, another of his familiar days.

Or rather, into an unfamiliar sort of day. Because when he felt in his left inside jacket pocket, where he used to keep whatever money he had managed to find or to earn, he noticed that all he had left was a fifty-franc note and some loose change. And at that, he, who for many years had not known the meaning of money, and had not been remotely interested in what it might mean – at that, he was taken aback, in the way that a man would be taken aback who expected to have money in his pocket at all times, and who suddenly found himself in the unwonted position of having very little. Suddenly, on the grey, empty pavement of early morning, he, who had had no money whatsoever for months, seemed to himself to have become poor because he didn't have quite as many notes in his pocket as he had had in the last couple of days. It seemed to him that the time of his impecuniousness was terribly remote, and that what he had done was to take the sum which should have been there to guarantee an appropriate standard of living for himself, and spend it recklessly and rather frivolously on Caroline.

It made him angry with Caroline. And all at once he, to whom the possession of money had never meant a thing, began to have a sense of what money was worth. All at once, he felt that the possession of a single fifty-franc note was demeaning to a man such as himself, and that, to appreciate his true worth again, he urgently needed to be able to reflect on the subject at leisure, and over a glass of Pernod.

He identified the most welcoming of the circumjacent hostelries, sat down and ordered a Pernod. Over his drink, he recalled that he was actually living in Paris without a residence permit, and he checked through his papers. And there he found that he had in fact been expelled from the country, because he had come to France as a coal-miner, from Olschowice in Polish Silesia.

6

Then, laying his tattered papers out on the table in front of him, he remembered that he had come here one day, many years ago, because he had read an announcement in the newspaper saying that they were looking for coal-miners in France. All his life he had longed to go to far-off places. And so he had gone to work in the mines at Quebecque, and he had sub-let a room from some compatriots of his, a married couple by the name of Shebiec. And he had fallen in love with the wife, and one day the husband had tried to kill her, and so he, Andreas, had killed the husband. Thereupon he had gone to prison for two years. The wife was Caroline.

All this was going through Andreas's head as he looked at his now invalid documents. And then he felt such unhappiness that he ordered another Pernod.

When he finally got up, he felt hungry, but it was hunger of a particular sort that only affects drunkards. It is a rather specialised type of craving (not for food at all) that only lasts for a few moments, and that can be immediately stilled if the person who suffers it imagines to himself the exact drink he feels like at that exact moment.

Andreas had long since forgotten his surname. But now, after he had been looking at his invalid papers, he remembered it. It was Kartak. His full name was Andreas Kartak. And he felt as though he had rediscovered himself after many years.

But he still felt a little angry with fate for making it impossible for him to earn any more money, by refusing to direct the fat, baby-faced man with the moustache to this café, when it had sent him to that other one. There is really nothing that people get used to so readily as miracles, once they have experienced them two or three times. Yes! In fact, such is human nature that people begin to feel betrayed when they don't keep getting all those things that a chance and fleeting circumstance once bestowed on them. People are like that – so why should Andreas be any different? He spent the rest of the day in various other establishments, and was soon quite reconciled to the fact that the age of miracles he had lately experienced was now, finally, at an end, and that the preceding age had resumed. And so, with his heart set on that slow decline for which a drunkard is always available – and which no sober person can possibly understand! – Andreas took himself back to the banks and bridges of the Seine.

There he slept, half in the daytime, half at night, as he had been used to doing for over a year, every so often managing to borrow a bottle of brandy from one or other of his *confrères* – until the Thursday night.

41

During the night he dreamed that St Thérèse came to him as a little girl with fair curls, and said to him: 'Why didn't you come and see me on Sunday?' And the little saint looked just the way he had imagined his own daughter would look, many years ago. And he had no daughter! And in his dream, he said to little Thérèse: 'That's no way to talk to me! Have you forgotten that I'm your father?' The girl answered: 'Sorry, father, but will you please, please come and see me on Sunday, the day after tomorrow, at Sainte Marie des Batignolles.'

On the morning after his dream, he rose refreshed, as he had done a week earlier, when the miracles were still happening to him, as though this dream was itself a miracle. He felt once more like going to the river and washing himself. But before taking off his jacket to that end, he looked in the left inside pocket, in the vague hope that there might still be some money there that he had perhaps overlooked. He reached into his jacket pocket, and while he didn't find any banknotes, there was still the leather wallet that he had bought some days earlier. He took it out. It really was extremely cheap and tatty — but what else could be expected from a second-hand one? Split leather. Cow's leather. He looked at it, because he could no longer remember having bought it, or when or where. How did I come by that? he asked himself. Finally he opened it, and saw that it had two compartments. Curious, he peered into both of them, and saw that one contained a banknote. He took it out. It was one thousand francs.

He put the thousand francs in his trouser pocket, and went down to the bank of the Seine, where, indifferent to being watched by any of his fellow-unfortunates, he washed his face, yes, and his neck too, almost joyfully. Then he put on his jacket again, and went out into the day, a day which he began by going into a *tabac* to buy cigarettes.

Now, he had enough change still left to pay for the cigarettes, but he didn't know when he would get a chance to change the one-thousand-franc bill that had so miraculously turned up in his wallet. Because he was still able to appreciate that in the eyes of the world, or in the eyes of those that have authority in the world, there was a considerable inconsistency between his clothes and his overall appearance, and the possession of a one-thousand-franc banknote. Nevertheless, heartened by this renewed miracle, he decided he would show the banknote. At the same time, drawing on the remains of his prudence, he would say to the man at the cash-till in the *tabac*: 'If you can't change a thousand francs, I've got it in change too. But I would be glad to have it changed.'

To Andreas's astonishment the patron of the *tabac* said: 'No, on the contrary! I need a one-thousand-franc note, and your coming is most opportune.' And the man changed the one thousand francs. Then Andreas stayed awhile at the bar of the *tabac*, and drank three glasses of white wine; an expression of his gratitude to fate for the miracle.

7

While he was standing at the bar, he noticed a framed drawing on the wall, behind the broad back of his host, and the drawing reminded him of an old school friend at Olschowice. He asked the patron: 'Who is that? I have a feeling I know him.' Thereupon the patron and the other customers standing at the bar all burst out laughing. 'What!' they shouted to one another. 'He doesn't know who that is!'

Because, of course, as any normal person would have

known, it was Kanjak, the great footballer from Silesia. But then how could a man who slept under bridges, an alcoholic like our Andreas, have known that? Feeling ashamed of himself anyway, particularly because he had just had his one-thousand-franc note changed, Andreas muttered: 'Of course I know him, he even happens to be a friend of mine. It's just not a terribly good likeness.' And, to avoid any further questions, he quickly paid and left.

Now, though, he was genuinely hungry. He made for the nearest restaurant, ate and drank red wine with his meal, had cheese and then coffee, and thought he would spend the afternoon at the cinema. Only he wasn't quite sure which one to go to. But knowing that he had as much money on him at that moment as any of the prosperous types passing him on the pavement, he headed for the great boulevards. Between the Opéra and the Boulevard des Capucines he looked for a film he might enjoy, and finally he found one. The poster advertising the film showed a man obviously bent on meeting his death in some far-distant adventure. It described him crawling through the desert under the searing rays of an implacable sun. That was the film for Andreas. He sat in the cinema, watching the man crossing the scorching desert. Andreas was just on the point of finding the hero an admirable character, and identifying with him, when the film abruptly took a happy turn, and the man in the desert was rescued by a passing caravan of scientific researchers, and whisked back to the cradle of European civilisation. Whereupon Andreas lost all respect for the hero. He was about to get up and leave when there appeared on the screen the image of the school friend whose picture he had seen a little earlier, behind the proprietor's back, when he had been propping up the bar. It was Kanjak the great footballer. Seeing him on the screen reminded Andreas that once, twenty years ago, he and Kanjak had shared a school bench, and he decided to make inquiries the next morning as to whether his old friend was presently in Paris.

For our Andreas had no less than nine hundred and eighty francs in his pocket.

And that is a not inconsiderable sum.

8

However, before he had even left the cinema, it occurred to him that there was actually no compelling reason why he should wait till tomorrow morning to find out the address of his friend and classmate; particularly in view of the rather large sum he had in his pocket.

Having so much money left had given Andreas such confidence that he decided to begin his inquiries for the address of his friend, the celebrated footballer Kanjak, right away, at the cashier's desk. He imagined he might perhaps have to go to the cinema manager to get an answer. But no! There was no one in all Paris so well known as the footballer Kanjak! Even the doorman knew where he lived. He lived in a hotel on the Champs Elysées. The doorman gave him its name; and our Andreas immediately set off there.

It was a small, quiet, distinguished hotel, just the sort of hotel where footballers and boxers, the elite of our time, like to live. Andreas felt rather odd as he stood in the foyer, and in the eyes of the hotel staff, he looked rather odd too. Still, they told him that the celebrated footballer Kanjak was at home, and was prepared to come down to the foyer straight away.

And come down he did, a couple of minutes later, and the two of them recognised each other right away. They began exchanging old memories of their schooldays even as they stood there, and then they went out to eat together, and there was great merriment between them.

They went out to eat together, and it so happened that the celebrated footballer asked his dissolute friend: 'Why are you looking so dissolute, and what are those rags you're wearing?'

'It would be a terrible thing,' replied Andreas, 'if I were to tell you how that came to pass. And it would greatly impair our mutual joy at this happy reunion of ours. So don't let's talk about that. Let's talk about more cheerful matters instead.'

'I've got an awful lot of suits,' said the celebrated footballer Kanjak, 'and I would be only too glad to let you have one of them. We shared a bench at school, and you let me copy your answers. What's a suit, compared to that! Where shall I have it sent?'

'You can't,' replied Andreas, 'because I haven't got an address. For some time now, I've been living under the bridges on the banks of the Seine.'

'Very well,' said the footballer Kanjak, 'in that case we'll rent a room for you, expressly so that I can give you a suit. Come along!'

When they had eaten, they went along, and the foot-baller Kanjak rented a room, and the price of it was twenty-five francs per day, and it was situated near the marvellous church in Paris that goes by the name of 'Madeleine'.

9

The room was on the fifth floor, and Andreas and the footballer had to take the lift up. Of course, Andreas had no luggage, but neither the porter nor the lift-boy nor anyone else on the hotel staff expressed any surprise at that. The whole thing was simply a miracle, and the nuts and bolts of a miracle have nothing miraculous about them. When they were both up in the room, the footballer Kanjak said to his former neighbour in class Andreas: 'I expect you need some soap.'

'Oh,' replied Andreas, 'I can get by without soap. I plan to stay here for a week without soap, but I'll still wash. But what I would like is for us to order something to drink, in honour of the room.'

And the footballer called for a bottle of cognac, which they emptied between them. Then they left the room, and took a taxi up to Montmartre, to the café where the girls sat, and which Andreas had only lately visited by himself. After sitting there for a couple of hours, exchanging memories of their schooldays, the footballer took Andreas home, that is, to the hotel room he had rented for him, and he said: 'It's late now. I'll leave you to yourself. Tomorrow I'll send you two suits. And – do you need money?'

'No,' said Andreas, 'I've got nine hundred and eighty francs, and that's a sizeable sum. You go home!'

'I'll drop round in a day or two,' said the footballer, his friend.

10

The room in which Andreas now found himself staying was number eighty-nine. As soon as he was alone, he sat down in the comfortable armchair, which was covered in pink rep, and began to take stock of his surroundings. First he looked at the red silk wall-covering, with its pattern of pale gold parrots' heads, then the door with three ivory doorknobs on its right hand side, the bedside table and the reading lamp on it with its dark green shade, and a second door, which had a white door-knob, that seemed to have something mysterious behind it, or mysterious at any rate to Andreas. In addition there was a black telephone by the bed, so handily placed that one could lie on the bed and reach across to pick up the receiver quite comfortably. After studying the room for a long time, intent on acquainting himself with it, Andreas suddenly felt a keen curiosity. The second door with the white doorknob irritated him, and in spite of his timidity and the fact that he was unaccustomed to the ways of hotel rooms, he got up, determined to see what it might open on to. He had naturally assumed it would be locked. How surprised he was to find that it opened easily, almost invitingly!

He saw before him a bathroom with gleaming tiles, and a tub white and shimmering, and a toilet, and, in short, what might have been termed in his circles a convenience.

At that moment he felt a pressing need to wash, and he turned on both the taps and filled the tub with hot and cold water. As he undressed to get into it, he regretted that he didn't have a change of shirt, because when he took off his shirt he saw that it was exceedingly dirty, and he already dreaded the moment when he would have to get out of the bath and back into his shirt.

He climbed into the bath, conscious of what a long time it was since he had last washed. He bathed gleefully, got out, got into his clothes, and then didn't know what to do with himself. More out of perplexity than curiosity, he opened the door of his room, went out into the corridor, and saw a woman on the point of leaving her room, as he had just done. She was young and beautiful. Indeed, she reminded him of the sales girl in the shop where he had bought his wallet, and also slightly of Caroline, and so he said hello to her and bowed, and when she nodded back to him, he felt emboldened and said to her straight out: 'I think you're beautiful.'

'I like you as well,' she replied, 'but now you must excuse me! Perhaps we'll see each other tomorrow.' And she disappeared down the dark corridor. He, though, suddenly in need of love, looked to see what the number was on her door.

It was number eighty-seven. He made a note of it in his heart.

11

He returned to his room and waited and listened. He felt absolutely determined not to wait till the morning to see the beautiful girl again. The almost uninterrupted stream of miracles of the last few days had convinced him that he must be in a state of grace; but by that same token, he believed himself entitled to a little excess of zeal on his own behalf, and he rather thought he would pre-empt grace, out of deference to it, as it were, and without causing it the slightest offence. So when he thought he could hear the quiet footfall of the girl from room eighty-seven in the corridor, he carefully opened the door of his room by a handsbreadth, and saw that it really was her, going back into her room. What he had failed to realise, though, as a consequence of long years of desuetude, was the by no means unimportant circumstance that the beautiful girl had observed his little act of espionage. Consequently, as profession and experience had taught her to do, she quickly produced a semblance of order in her room, switched off the main overhead light, lay down on the bed and picked up a book and began reading it; unfortunately it was a book she had already read long ago.

A few moments later, as expected, she heard a quiet knock on her door, and Andreas stepped into her room. He remained standing by the door, merely awaiting the invitation to step a little closer which he was sure would not be long in coming. However, the pretty girl didn't move; she didn't even put her book aside, she only asked: 'And what brings you here?'

Andreas, his confidence boosted by bath, soap, arm-chair, wall-covering, parrots' heads and suit, replied: 'I couldn't wait till tomorrow to see you again, my dear.'

The girl made no reply.

Andreas moved a little nearer, asked what she was reading and observed with frankness: 'Books don't interest me.'

'I'm passing through,' said the girl on the bed, 'I'm only staying till Sunday. On Monday I have to appear in Cannes.'

'As what?' asked Andreas.

'I dance in a night-club. I'm Gabby. Haven't you ever heard of me?'

'Of course, I've seen your name in the newspapers,' lied Andreas — and he was even going to add: the newspapers I sleep in. But he didn't.

He sat down on the edge of the bed, and the pretty girl didn't object. She eventually put away her book, and Andreas stayed in room eighty-seven till morning.

12

On the Saturday morning, he awoke with the firm resolve not to leave the beautiful girl until it was time for her to go. Yes, and the fragrant thought bloomed in his mind that he might even travel down to Cannes with her, because, like all poor people (and more especially, like all poor people who also drink), he was inclined to take the small sums of money in his pocket for large ones. So, in the morning, he counted up his nine hundred and eighty francs. And since they were in a wallet, and the wallet was in a new suit, the sum seemed to him to be ten times what it actually was. As a result, he wasn't at all put out when, an hour after he'd left her, the pretty girl walked straight into his room without knocking, and, when she asked him how they would spend their Saturday together, he said, at a venture, 'Fontainebleau.' It was like a name he had heard in a dream. He had no idea how and why it came to trip off his tongue now.

So they took a taxi and drove out to Fontainebleau, and it turned out that the beautiful girl knew of a good restaurant, where they served good food and fine wines. And the waiter there knew her, and she was on first name terms with him. And if our Andreas had been of a jealous disposition, it might have made him angry. But he wasn't jealous, and so he didn't get angry. They spent some time eating and drinking, and then they drove back to Paris, again in a taxi, and suddenly they saw the glittering expanse of the evening in Paris ahead of them, and they didn't know what to do with it, and they were just two people who didn't belong together, whom fate had simply thrown together. The night stretched out ahead of them like an empty desert.

And they were at a loss what to do together, having rather frivolously squandered the principal experience that a man and woman may have together. And so they decided to avail themselves of the facility reserved to people in our own century when they don't know what to do – they went to the cinema. And they sat there, and it wasn't pitch-black, it wasn't even dark, in fact it could barely be called half-dark. And they held hands, the girl and our friend Andreas. But his hand felt non-committal, and it embarrassed him. His own hand. When the interval came, he decided to take the beautiful girl out into the foyer for a drink, and they went out and they drank. And he had no interest whatever in the film any more. They went back to their hotel feeling awkward and constrained.

The following morning, the Sunday, Andreas woke up fully aware of his obligation to repay the money. He got up rather more quickly than he had done on the previous morning, with such alacrity in fact that the beautiful girl

73

was startled out of her sleep, and asked, 'Why the hurry, Andreas?'

'I have a debt to repay,' said Andreas.

'What? Today? On a Sunday?' asked the beautiful girl.

'Yes, today, Sunday,' replied Andreas.

'Is it a man or a woman you owe money to?'

'A woman,' said Andreas, a little hesitantly.

'What's her name?'

'Thérèse.'

Thereupon the beautiful girl leapt out of bed, clenched both her fists and started pummelling Andreas with them.

He fled the room, left the hotel, and, without any further deviation, made straight for Sainte Marie des Batignolles, completely confident that today at last he would be able to repay little Thérèse her two hundred francs.

13

Now, as providence would have it — or, as less devout people would say, luck — Andreas once more arrived just too late for the ten o'clock Mass. And, not unnaturally, he once again caught sight of the bistro across the square, where he had gone to drink on the previous occasion, and it was there that he went this time as well.

He ordered a drink. But, canny man that he was, as all the poor people in the world are canny, even after they have been showered with one miracle after another, he first checked the state of his wallet, and took it out of his breast pocket. And he saw that his nine hundred and eighty francs were almost completely gone.

He had only two hundred and fifty left. He thought awhile, and realised that the beautiful girl in the hotel must have taken his money. But our Andreas wasn't at all upset by that. He told himself that enjoyment had to be paid for, that he had enjoyed himself, and that he therefore had had to pay.

He wanted to wait here until he heard the bells, the church bells ringing people to Mass, before crossing the square and settling his debt to the little saint. But until then he wanted to drink, and he ordered something to drink. He drank. The bells began to ring, summoning people to Mass, and he called, 'Waiter, the bill please!' and he paid, got up, went out, and just outside the door he collided with a very tall broad-shouldered man. 'Wojtech!' he cried instantly. And the other, just as quickly: 'Andreas!' They fell into

78

one another's arms, because they had been miners together in Quebecque, both of them working in the same pit.

'Why don't you wait here till I come back,' said Andreas, 'I'll be twenty minutes, just as long as Mass takes, not a moment longer!'

'Not a bit of it,' said Wojtech. 'When did you start going to Mass anyway? If there's anyone I hate more than priests, it's the people who go to them.'

'But I'm going to little Thérèse,' said Andreas, 'I owe her some money.'

'Do you mean little St Thérèse?' asked Wojtech.

'Yes, her,' replied Andreas.

'How much do you owe her?' asked Wojtech.

'Two hundred francs!' said Andreas.

'In that case I'll go with you!' said Wojtech.

The bells were still ringing. They went into the church and as they stood in the aisle, and Mass was just beginning, Wojtech hissed: 'Give me a hundred francs, will you! I've just remembered that there's someone waiting for me outside, otherwise he'll have me put away!'

Andreas immediately handed over both of the hundred-franc notes he had, and said: 'I'll see you out there in a minute.'

But when it dawned on him that he no longer had the money with which to repay Thérèse, it seemed pointless to him to spend any more time at Mass. Forbearance alone kept him there for another five minutes, then he went back over to the bistro where he found Wojtech waiting for him.

From that moment on, as they assured one another, they were best mates.

In fact, Wojtech didn't have a friend waiting outside, to whom he owed money. He took one of the two hundred-franc notes that Andreas had lent him, and carefully wrapped it in his handkerchief and knotted it up. With the other one, he bought him a drink, and another, and another, and in the evening they went to the house where the obliging girls roosted, and they holed up there for two days, and when they emerged again, it was Tuesday, and Wojtech took leave of Andreas with the words: 'Let's meet up again on Sunday, same time, same place.'

'See you then!' said Andreas.

'See you!' said Wojtech, and vanished.

14

It was a rainy Tuesday afternoon, and the rain was so heavy that, a moment later, Wojtech had actually vanished. Or at least so it seemed to Andreas. It seemed to him that he had lost his friend in the rain, just as he had chanced to bump into him earlier, and since he only had thirty-five francs left, and believing himself to be fortune's spoilt darling, and fully confident of further miracles, he decided, like all poor men and habitual drinkers, to entrust himself to god, to the only god he believed in. So he went back down the familiar steps, back down to the Seine, to the home of all the homeless vagrants.

There he bumped into a man who was just about to go up the steps, and who struck him as familiar. Accordingly, Andreas greeted him with great politeness. The elderly, spruce gentleman stopped, looked closely at Andreas and finally asked: 'My dear chap, do you need any money?'

Andreas recognised the voice of the gentleman he had met two weeks previously in the same place. So he replied: 'I know full well I still owe you money, and I promised to take it along to St Thérèse. But you see, things kept cropping up. In fact, I've already made two attempts to pay the money back.'

'There must be some mistake,' said the elderly, well-dressed gentleman, 'I don't have the honour of your acquaintance. You must have mistaken me for someone else, but it looks to me as though you're in a spot of difficulty. Now, you mentioned St Thérèse, and you must know that I am personally so devoted to her that I am naturally prepared to advance you whatever sum you owe her. What is the sum, if you please?'

'Two hundred francs,' replied Andreas, 'but honestly, you don't know me! I'm a man of my word, and you'll hardly be able to send me a bill. I have my honour, but I have no address. Each night I sleep under one of these bridges.'

'Oh, that's all right!' said the gentleman. 'That's where I sleep too. In accepting this money from me, you'll be doing me a favour for which I shan't be able to thank you enough. Because I too am so beholden to little Thérèse!'

'In that case,' said Andreas, 'consider me at your disposal.'

He took the money, waited till the gentleman had climbed the steps, and then he climbed up to the quay himself and went directly to the Rue des Quatre Vents, to his old haunt, the Russian-Armenian restaurant Tari-Bari, where he stayed until Saturday night. He then remembered that the following day was Sunday, and that he had an assignation at the church of Sainte Marie des Batignolles.

15

The Tari-Bari was crowded, because many clochards would put up there for days, sleeping behind the bar by day, and on the benches at night. Andreas got up very early on Sunday, less to be sure of arriving in time for Mass, than for fear that the landlord would demand payment from him for drink and food and lodging for so many days.

But he miscalculated, because the landlord had got up even earlier than he had. The landlord had known him a long time, and so he knew that our Andreas was inclined to take every opportunity of avoiding paying his bills. And so our Andreas was made to pay, from Tuesday till Sunday, for a lot of food and drink, in fact for rather more than he had personally consumed. For the landlord of the Tari-Bari was able to distinguish between those of his customers who were numerate and those who weren't. And our Andreas, like many drinkers, belonged to the category of the latter. Therefore he paid a great part of the money he had, and then, nothing daunted, set off for the Chapelle de Sainte Marie des Batignolles. He realised, though, that he no longer had enough money to repay Thérèse. But in fact his thoughts were as much on his rendezvous with his friend Wojtech, as on his little creditress.

So he reached the neighbourhood of the church, and unfortunately he was once again late for the ten o'clock Mass, and once again people streamed past him out of the church, and when he once again turned aside to go to the bistro, he heard a shout behind him, and felt a rough hand descend on his shoulder. He turned round, and saw that it was a policeman's.

At this our Andreas, who, as we know, had no valid papers, like many of his ilk, was frightened, and he reached into his pocket to give at least the illusion that he might have some valid papers there. But the policeman said: 'I know what you're looking for. But you won't find it in your pocket! You've just dropped your wallet. Here it is, and,' he added good-naturedly, 'remember that's what comes of drinking so many aperitifs so early on a Sunday morning! . . .'

Andreas quickly took the wallet; he barely had the presence of mind to tip his hat to the policeman in gratitude, and swiftly dived into the bistro.

He found Wojtech already there, though it took him a while to recognise him, so that when he finally did so, he greeted him with relief and fervour. Then each man simply wouldn't stop taking it in turn to buy the other a drink, and Wojtech, a polite fellow like the majority of mankind, got up from the bench, gave Andreas pride of place on it, and staggeringly circum-navigated the table and sat down on a chair opposite him, chatting away to him politely. They drank nothing but Pernod.

'Something peculiar happened to me again,' said Andreas. 'As I'm on my way to our rendezvous, a police-man taps me on the shoulder and says: "You've lost your wallet." And he hands me one that doesn't even belong to me, and I take it, and now I want to have a look and see what I've been given.'

And he takes out the wallet and looks at it, and there are various bits of paper in it that he doesn't bother about, and he sees there's some money in it too, and he counts the bills, and they come to exactly two hundred francs. And Andreas says: 'You see! It's a sign from the Almighty! Now I'm going to go over there and pay my debt at last!'

'That,' said Wojtech, 'can wait till Mass is over. What do you need Mass for? You can't pay the money back while Mass is going on. Go along to the vestry when it's over, and until then we can sit here and drink!'

'All right,' replied Andreas, 'whatever you say.'

Just at that moment the door opened, and Andreas felt a lightness in his head and a terrible pang in his heart when he saw a girl come in and sit down on the bench directly opposite him. She was very young, younger than any girl he'd ever seen, and she was dressed entirely in sky blue. She was as blue as only the sky can be, and then only on certain blessed days.

So he staggered across to her, bowed and said to the little girl: 'What are you doing here?'

'I'm waiting for my parents to come out of Mass; they're meeting me here. Every fourth Sunday,' she said, and was quite abashed by the older man who had suddenly come over and started speaking to her. She was a bit afraid of him.

Andreas asked: 'What's your name?'

'Thérèse,' she said.

'Ah,' cried Andreas, 'that's lovely! I never thought that such a great little saint, such a great little creditress would do me the honour of coming to me after I've failed to go to her for such a long time.'

93

'I don't understand you,' said the little miss, who was rather bewildered by this.

'That's just your civility,' Andreas replied. 'That's just your civility, but I recognise it for what it is. I've owed you two hundred francs for a long time, and I didn't manage to get to you and pay them back, holy miss!'

'You don't owe me any money, but I've got some in my purse – please take it and leave me alone. My parents are going to be here any minute.'

And she gave him a hundred-franc note from her purse.

Wojtech was watching all this in the mirror, and he got up out of his chair, ordered a couple of Pernods, and was on the point of dragging Andreas up to the bar to drink them with him. But just as Andreas gets up to go to the bar, he collapses on the floor like a sack, and everyone in the bistro is alarmed, including Wojtech, and the little girl most of all. And because there is no doctor close at hand, and no chemist's shop, he is dragged across the square to the church, to the vestry in fact, because even the unbelieving waiters believe that priests know something about living and dying; and the girl called Thérèse, she too accompanies them.

So they bring our poor Andreas into the vestry, and unfortunately he's no longer capable of speech, all he can do is reach for the left inside pocket of his jacket where he has the money he owes his little creditress, and he says: 'Miss Thérèse!' – and he sighs once, and he dies.

May God grant us all, all of us drinkers, such a good and easy death!

Translator's Note

*T*he *Legend of the Holy Drinker* is Joseph Roth's last work of fiction, quite deliberately so. Like Andreas's repayment of the two hundred francs, it was his last detail. Again like Andreas, he took his time over it, didn't rush — as most of his books were rushed — but worked at it slowly, with pleasure and pride, for the first four months of 1939. At the end of the fifth, he died. He was not quite forty-five years old.

It is an invidious thing to knock away the props of a

dead man, but it is clear that Roth for some time had been running out of reasons to remain alive. Being an exiled writer was attritional, and beyond that, it was perspectiveless. Politically, economically, emotionally and physically he was under threat. Alcoholism had destroyed his health; in 1938 he suffered a heart attack, and he could walk no more than a few steps. He advanced a sophisticated argument that while drink shortened his life in the medium term, in the short term it kept him alive – and he worked hard at testing its logic. After his beloved Hôtel Foyot was pulled down in 1937 (for twelve years it had been 'home' to this inveterate and committed hotel-dweller), he moved to the Hôtel de la Poste, above the Café Tournon. His attic room was so tiny that he would fall out of bed straight into the corridor, and thence plunge downstairs into the bar. There he would spend the rest of the day and all night holding court, working, and, increasingly, drinking and brooding beside a small Babel of saucers. His friends and colleagues were dying, often in grotesque circumstances. In 1938, he went to Horváth's funeral, and told friends that the next obituary they would write would be his own. It was the news of another friend's death, the suicide of the playwright Ernst Toller, that precipitated his own collapse, hospitalisation and death after four days of bungled treatment.

In the circumstances, it is miraculous that Roth should still have been able to write anything at all, doubly miraculous that it should have come out as light and elegant and sparkling as *The Legend of the Holy Drinker*. The word 'legend' is rather soggy in English, but the first dictionary definition of it is 'the life of a saint', and Andreas is indeed the unlikeliest of saints. But there are many unlikely saints, and Andreas is as much imbued with hope, faith and charity as the best of them. A merciful irony plays over Andreas — the irony of a loving god who drinks, and who can understand his 'hunger', his courtliness, his choice of hostelry, his behaviour in the ritzy hotel room. Drink in the book is a philosophy, almost a formal device (as in farce); it is certainly not content, still less milieu. A drinker's blackouts, confusions and carelessness — or liberality — are a way of experiencing the world. The suggestion throughout is, to say it with Robert Frost, 'One could do worse.'

It is customary — and usually correct — to praise Roth's style for its simplicity. But Roth is not monosyllabic and not Hemingway. He is a thoughtful, quirky and refined writer. Simplicity in English is apt to be taken for rawness, simple-mindedness or blandness, and Roth is very far from being any of these. Nor would he have allowed simplicity to obstruct him in what he was saying. Therefore, after little hesitation, I have decided to plump for a style that gives expression to Roth's ironic capacity, flexibility and qualities of thought. In English, this means using French and Latin words, and this I have very occasionally done, conscious all the time that Roth would have deplored such a practice (and even more the condition of the language that necessitates it), but thinking that in the end he too would have had to adopt it.

Michael Hofmann
November 1988, London